Ghost of Shandon

Alan Corbett

What sound is that, it comes from afar?
Still rolling and rumbling, that sound
Makes nearer and nearer approach,
Do I tremble, or is it the ground?
Lord save us! What is it?

-The Death Coach

First Edition

A PLAN *of the City of* CORK
as in the Year 1750

D. Corbett. *Sculp.*

Road to You...
Key's Well Street
Sand Quay
Mallow Lane
New Quay
Peter's Lane
Fair Lane
Hammand's Fields
Shandon Street
Old Mark...
Shamble
St. Frances Abby
Shandon's Crook Lane
North Quay
Back Lane
Knappas Lane
RIVER LEE
RIVER LEE
Georges Key Quay
Lewis's Quay
Bow Hill Lane
Brown's Str...
Harper's Lane
Newmans Quay
Potatoe Quay
Lavitts Lane
Main - Street
Gate
Batchelors Quay
Hammonds Mar...
Assembly...
Howling Green
RIVER LEE

25   24   31   33   35

10   9   8
11   7
29   19
21

1. Poor House
2. Infirmary
3. Green Boys Hos...
4. St. Anne's Chura...
5. Shandon Castle
6. Shandon Church
7. Bridewell
8. Custom House
9. St. Paul's Church

2

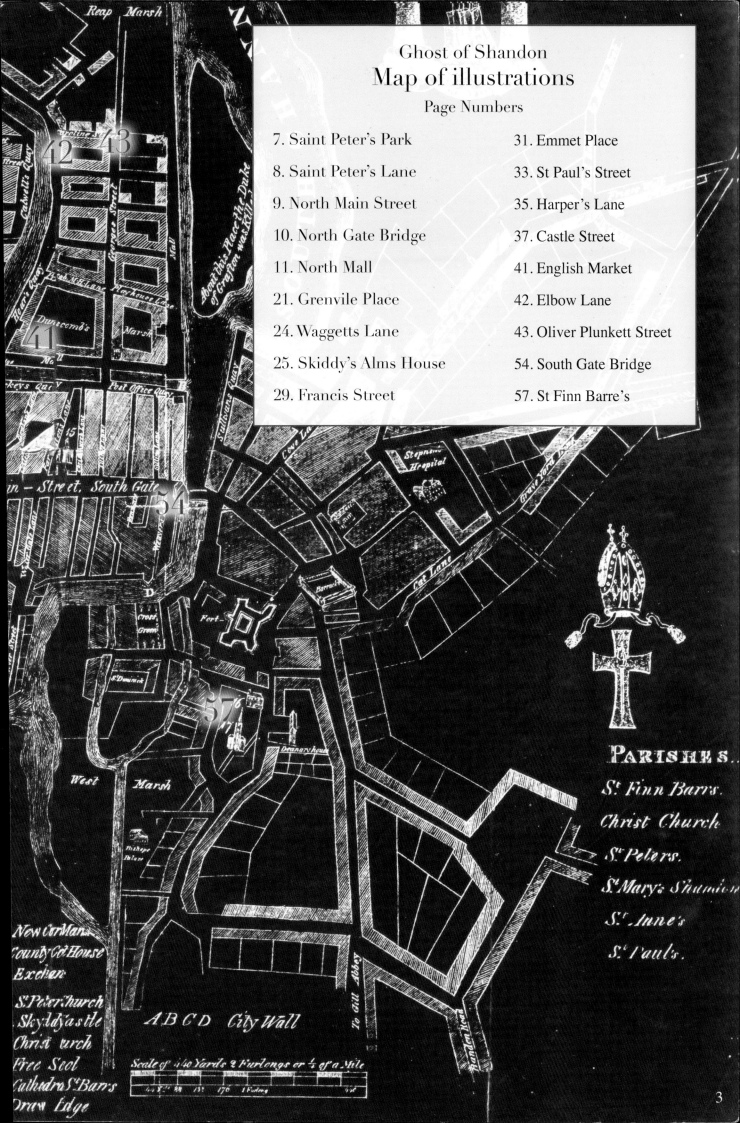

Ghost of Shandon
Map of illustrations
Page Numbers

PARISHES.

St Finn Barrs.
Christ Church
St Peters.
St Mary's Shandon
St Anne's
St Pauls.

PRESENT DAY CORK CITY

The school bell rang and the pupils rushed out the main gates of Saint Kevin's. It had been another terrible day at school for Ronan.

Vincent and his friends threw scrumpled paper at poor Ronan...

WHACK!

...as he ran off down the street. Alone.

Ronan hid away as he usually did after school in Saint Peter's Park.

Saint Peter's Park

Vincent was making Ronan's school life a miserable one and his dad wouldn't be home from work for another hour or so.

Ronan tried his best to escape from this horrible reality by reading from his favourite book, The Three Musketeers.

Ronan was very lonely. Even though he was living in the middle of a busy and bustling city like Cork, he still felt like the loneliest boy in the world. Things simply could not get much worse...

What are you doing there, boy? A graveyard is no place to sit around reading!

That was, of course, until Aisling turned up.

Do you not have any respect for the dead?

Ronan stared at the headstones that lined the wall of Saint Peter's Park. He had never taken much notice before but there was definitely something different about them today. They looked like new, all clean and tidy, unlike the moss-covered and neglected graves he was used to. The lettering was clearly visible too. He looked at one: Charles Besnard, Passed Away August 4th, 1792.

Come with me Ronan the faerie, the apothecary will know what to do with you. I'm sure to get a reward for capturing a mischievous creature like yourself, lurking in a graveyard!

But what is an apothecary?

You've never heard of an apothecary? You are a strange creature. An apothecary is a man who makes potions to cure illness. He'll know all about faeries like you.

Ronan didn't really have any choice in the matter as Aisling took him by the hand and marched him down the narrow alley that led beyond Saint Peter's Church.

Saint Peter's Lane

Ronan broke free of Aisling's hand and ran out onto nearby North Main Street. He stopped still in shock: everything had changed. Tall chimneys rose into the sky above thatched and purple-tiled rooftops. Oddly dressed men in colourful cloaks talked with strange foreign accents.

Women in shawls scurried about carrying baskets of bread from the busy market stalls and the children played barefoot on the muddied, cobbled street. The smells of buttermilk and burning turf wafted through the air. Ronan couldn't believe his eyes as a man on horseback rode up the street.

Ronan and Aisling approached the tall, gloomy building of the apothecary.

It was damp and dark inside. The blue windows made it feel like the inside of a glass bottle. Jars with cocktails of all colours and textures glinted on every shelf. Stark, white, staring animal skulls hung from the ceiling. Behind the counter, with his scientific instuments and equipment, lurched the master apothecary himself.

The Apothecary of Victor Wolfe

Victor Wolfe crouched down and inspected Ronan's eyes and mouth. His beady yellow eyes studied Ronan's face and his long nails pressed into the boy's skull. Ronan could hardly breathe with the strong smell of vinegar that came from Wolfe.

Of course I can talk, my name is Ronan and I told Aisling already, I'm no faerie.

Ardnakinna Lighthouse

I was born and raised at Ardnakinna Lighthouse in Castletownbere.

Four days after my eighth birthday, the lighthouse was closed down and myself and my dad had to move into Cork City. I don't belong here, I belong in the 21st Century!

Well, Ronan the faerie, I think I believe you but I'm afraid I still have some very bad news for you. If you really have travelled back in time there's no way to return … unless, that is of course, you believe in the legend.

What legend?

The legend goes that to travel out of this time, a faerie needs three things: firstly a drop of an ancient potion made from the water of the Dead Sea. This must fall on the keys to the city which must be then turned in the city's oldest doors, where Cork began in the 7th Century, at St Finn Barre's Cathedral.

The name of the potion is Artasian and it must come all the way from Constantinople. It is said to give metal the power to unlock the faerie world.

It was a well known fact in Cork that a secret group of wealthy merchants and law officials called the Friendly Club ran the city. Nobody knew exactly who the members of the Friendly Club were, though everyone thought the mayor, Vesian Pick, was probably a member. The Friendly Club met in a secret location in the city. Wolfe told Ronan he had always suspected the keys to the city could be found there.

But be warned Ronan, if you truly have broken through time and entered the past, there is no reason that darker, more sinister faeries might not have followed you.

The Tale of the Dualachan was a frightening one that had been terrorising the people of Cork City for years. The Dualachan was said to be a dark faerie that raced through the land from the churchyard of Rathcooney out to the Old Head of Kinsale. It had no face or eyes to call its own so it would search desperately, hunting for the eyes of lost souls.

Every midnight, it raced through the land from the churchyard of Rathcooney out to the Old Head of Kinsale.

Rathcooney Graveyard

Oh yes, the malicious goblin Dualachan would undoubtedly love to lay his hands on a changeling faerie like you, but don't worry, you can trust me. I'll help you on your passage home.

If you find the keys to the city, bring them to me and I will give you the Artasian potion to unlock the doors of St Fin Barre's Cathedral.

There will be a reward for you too, Aisling, if you help this faerie return home. I always look after my own, isn't that right my girl?

Aisling and Ronan took Wolfe's advice and decided to spy on the mayor. They made their way through the narrow lane ways of Cork City to the Mansion House.

Francis Street

A merchant sailor was waiting with a carriage and trailer full of turtles. Suddenly, the doors of the Mansion House burst open and out stumbled the mayor, Vesian Pick, to greet the sailor.

Pick was a Huguenot merchant from France who had settled in Cork and became mayor in 1779. He was a plump man with a black moustache that curled under his nose.

My good man, what is it that you have here for me?

Ronan and Aisling crouched down behind empty wine barrels outside the mayor's house.

23

Aisling told Ronan how she had only gone to school for a very short while. In fact she was very lucky to have spent anytime at all there.

She went to the Green Coats School in Shandon for a couple of months but her time there didn't last long.

Green Coats School

Tuckey's House

She was then employed by Dutch merchants, the Tuckey family, to work as a maid.

When she was younger, the Lady with the Lantern, Nano Nagle, had found Aisling sick and begging on Waggetts Lane. Nano Nagle was famous throughout the city. She was a close friend of the Tuckeys and was very well respected for looking after the poor and sick, especially children.

Waggetts Lane

Skiddy's Alms House

St. Anne's

Nano Nagle had brought Aisling to Skiddy's Almshouse in Shandon, a hospital mostly for retired soldiers and navy men.

Aisling had been very sick as a child and spent a great deal of time trying to get better at the almshouse.

She was one of the few children there . Every day she would listen to the stories and tales of the retired soldiers and sailors who gathered to talk about their adventures on the high seas and the notorious pirates of the Atlantic ocean.

Her favourite stories were of the infamous female pirate Anne Bonny from Kinsale in Cork. Across the length and breadth of the ocean, all the way from Spain to the Caribbean, Anne Bonny was feared.

Pirate Ship Revenge

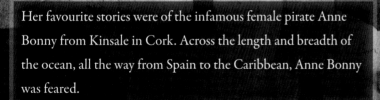

Aisling would practise her duelling skills for hours on end using discarded walking sticks and crutches. Nothing felt better to Aisling than to grip a crutch like a sword and wave it about like a battle ready soldier, imagining she was confronting Anne Bonny under the blazing sun of the Caribbean.

Aisling enjoyed Skiddy's and was eager to learn. She was eventually moved into the nearby Green Coat School to sample what a proper education was like...

Before the Tuckey family came along and decided for her that she should spend her life as a maid.

Still, adventure was in Aisling's blood and she longed for the day when she could sneak aboard a navy ship at Cork harbour and prove to the world what a great soldier she could be.

We're going to have to try and sneak into the Theatre Royal tonight, to the masked ball, maybe there'll be a meeting of the Friendly Club there.

Aisling was beginning to drift off thinking about Anne Bonny when Ronan shook her arm to wake her up and remind her of the task at hand.

Well sneaking into the Theatre Royal wont be easy. We're going to have to figure out a way of getting disguises. Maybe we could try the Custom House?

The Doll's House

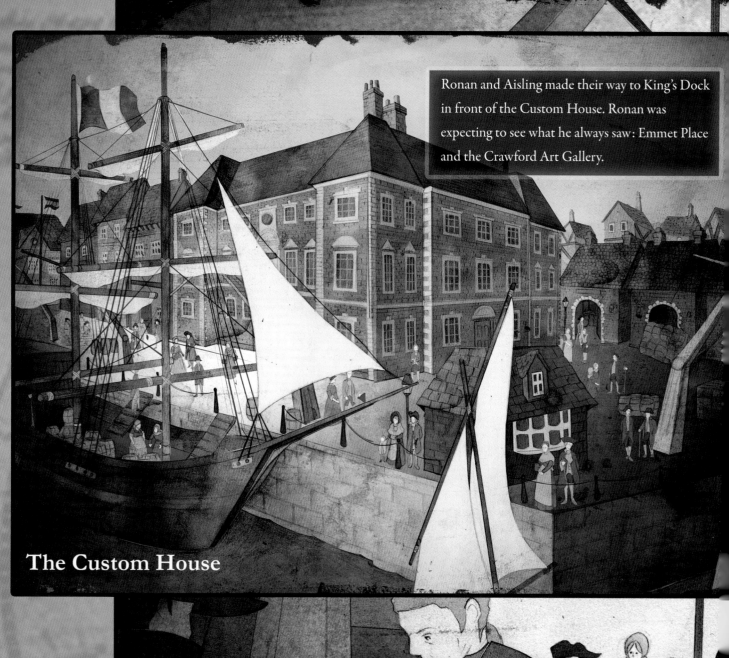

Ronan and Aisling made their way to King's Dock in front of the Custom House. Ronan was expecting to see what he always saw: Emmet Place and the Crawford Art Gallery.

The Custom House

Instead, he was confronted with tall ships docked in the harbour and cranes rising high into the sky, pulling cargo onto the dock. Ledgers scurried about recording merchant and trader ship numbers and signage. Aisling approached a ledger who was taking records of new cargo to ask about unwanted clothing.

King's Dock

33

Once they selected their clothes, the pair made their way through what Ronan knew as the Huguenot Quarter and back towards the Tuckey family home on Francis Street.

As they made their way through Paul Street, Aisling stopped still in utter shock and horror. Ronan looked ahead of him, but all he could see were the uneven buildings on Castle Street and the Corn Exchange.

What's wrong Aisling? What's happening?

Don't move Ronan! To your right … it's the Dualachan!

Ronan turned slowly down Harper's Lane and there it was, the dark sinister figure of the Dualachan. He had no mouth or nose or any facial features at all, just the deepest black hollows where his eyes should be. He sat high on his mighty black stallion which pulled along the death coach.

Do you believe in faeries now Ronan?

Harper's Lane

Dualachan's death coach burst into life and sped down the narrow alley after them.

DUALACHAN!!!

Run Aisling!

Ronan and Aisling raced past the Coal Quay Market and Castle Street towards the Tuckey family home.

Castle Street

39

Not for one second did they look behind to see if the Dualachan was catching up.

They raced through the front door of the Tuckey's house and slammed it behind them, They collapsed onto the floor gasping for breath.

That was close!

They picked up their dirty disguises and scurried down the steps of the cellar. Aisling immediately began washing the salvaged clothing. Ronan poured in some old perfume from Tuckey's shop into the washing tub.

CTHODS OF PREPARING

They talked about the terrifying Dualachan. How would they go about sneaking into the Theatre Royal tonight? Would they be lucky enough to find a Friendly Club meeting in full swing?

They were both very nervous, but their determination and spirit were too strong to give up at this stage. They just needed to get some masks at the English Market for the ball. Aisling came up with the great idea of using some of the old perfume stored in the house to trade for masks.

The pair made their way to the English Market dressed as two well-to-do gentlemen carrying a basket of perfumes.

Grand Parade

Ronan and Aisling hurried down the narrow Elbow Lane towards the Theatre Royal.

Elbow Lane

A huge crowd had gathered outside the theatre, many wearing masks. There was a wonderful carnival atmosphere with people dancing and cheering. Ronan had never experienced anything like the excitement outside the theatre.

Ronan mentioned to Aisling that he only ever saw people wore masks for Hallowe'en night!

The cheers got louder and louder when the Theatre Royal owner Spranger Barry arrived. It became apparent after his name was cheered roundly that John Butts, the renowned Cork artist, was tonight's special guest.

To add to the excitement Butts was carrying a new painting under his arm.

Ronan and Aisling darted behind the guard of honour and into the theatre.

Her wonderful voice bellowed the Italian lyrics across the theatre space. Aisling knew if there was going to be a Friendly Club meeting it would have to be upstairs, away from the noise of the stage.

Spranger and Butts entered the Theatre Royal with a group of waiters scurrying behind them, carrying turtle soup and bottles of wine.

Aisling caught Ronan by the hand and they managed to rush up the stairs, hidden between the servants. Aisling knew the turtle soup was for Mayor Vesian Pick.

The group entered a large banquet hall where six of the most important men in the city sat around a huge table headed by Pick, There was Admiral Drury, Sheriff Thomas Gibbings, the Surgeon William Charles Callow and the two Huguenot merchants, Julius Besnard and David Perrier. It had to be the Friendly Club.

The Friendly Club

Suddenly the doors to the banquet hall burst open and there stood the horrifying figure of the shadowy Dualachan!

The Dualachan?
Afraid not.
No, I'm much worse than that.

Standing back in astonishment, the Friendly Club watched as the dark figure grabbed Ronan.

Fear me.
I'm the apothecary Victor Wolfe. Hand over the keys to the city and I won't harm this stupid boy. It's about time the people of this city knew what real terror is like.

Victor Wolfe snatched the key from Callow's hand and charged out of the Theatre Royal with his hostage. He threw Ronan into the back of the death coach, smacked his horse with his whip and stormed away from the theatre.

The death coach thundered its way across South Gate Bridge with Ronan tied up inside. The admiral and Aisling chased in hot pursuit until they reached the gates of St Fin Barre's!

South Gate Bridge

St. Finn Barre's

Victor was there before them. In front of the great doors of the cathedral he pulled Ronan out from the coach and threw him to the ground like a rag doll.

Stop right there Wolfe, the so called apothecary that you are!

How dare you Admiral! You're nothing but a pup in the uniform of a soldier!

The boy is entirely innocent and we both know why you're really here, don't we, or should I refer to you as Captain de la Hyde? You might be good at creating your disguises, William, but in the end, your real colours will always shine through!

Ronan and Aisling watched in horror as Admiral Drury and Wolfe locked swords in the courtyard. A great and ferocious battle ensued. The clatter of swords could be heard across the River Lee.

I assure you Admiral, I am no poser of magic, my alchemy is more powerful than you could ever be!

Wolfe unveiled his alchemy potion, the Artasian, and threw it in the eyes of Admiral Drury.

The admiral fell to the ground and Wolfe leered over his strucken foe, ready to strike the final blow.

Aisling grabbed the admiral's sword and leapt to his rescue. The swords of the apothecary and Aisling clashed in the twilight. With a skilled swipe from left to right, Aisling lifted Wolfe's sword upwards and out of his grip. It landed well out of his reach and Aisling stood strong and victorious.

Ronan had only ever read of such battles in books like The Three Musketeers and there Aisling stood, more musketeer than anything he had ever dreamt of.